Headgear

Written by Jo Windsor

In this book you will see headgear.

You will see headgear like this:

helmet

glasses

lights

Look at this woman.
She is skiing.

She is going very *fast*.

Look at her headgear.
It is a helmet.

The helmet is to...
keep her head safe   Yes? No?
make her go fast   Yes? No?

helmet

This is a bike race.

The bikes are
going very *fast*.

Look out!
Look out!

The people have crashed!
The helmets help
keep them safe.

helmets

This woman is playing hockey on the ice.

Look at her headgear.

It is a helmet.
The helmet will keep her head safe.

The headgear is to...

keep her eyes safe   Yes? No?

keep her mouth safe   Yes? No?

helmet

The people are building.

They have headgear, too.

The helmets will keep their heads safe.

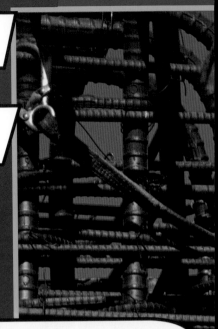

Headgear can be for...

people building houses Yes? No?

people having dinner Yes? No?

This headgear has lights.

The men are under the ground.

The lights will help them see.

The headgear will...

help the men work   Yes? No?

keep their heads safe   Yes? No?

light →

Look at all the *sparks.*

The people are working.

The *sparks* will not get into their eyes.

They have helmets to keep their eyes safe.

helmet

The people are under the water.

Their headgear keeps their heads warm.

The headgear helps them get air, too.

Headgear for people under the water:

Yes? No?   Yes? No?   Yes? No?

This man is in space.

He has headgear
to keep him safe.

There is no air in space.
This helmet helps the
man get air.

**The headgear helps
the man...**

get air   Yes? No?

see   Yes? No?

sleep   Yes? No?

helmet

Here are two doctors.

The doctors are working.
The glasses on their heads
help them see.

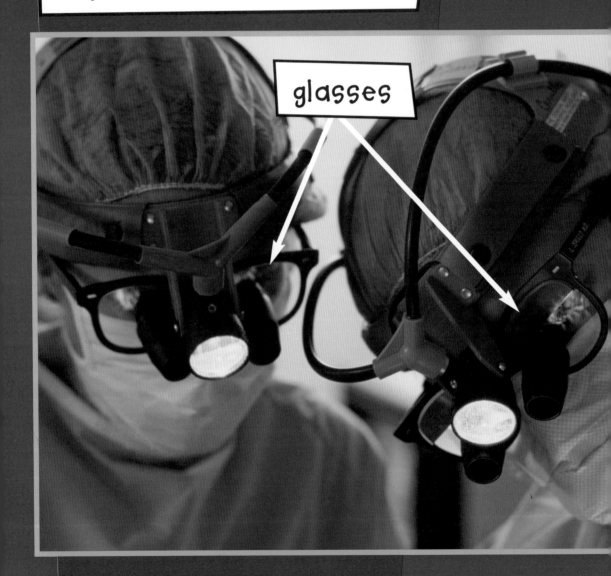

glasses

Index

headgear

    for a bike race 6

    for hockey 8

    for skiing 4

    for space 18

    for under the water . .16

    for working 10, 12, 14, 20

A yes/no chart

Headgear to keep you safe

sunhat  **Yes? No?**

glasses  **Yes? No?**

nose  **Yes? No?**

cook's hat  **Yes? No?**

goggles  Yes? No?

mask  Yes? No?

sweatbands 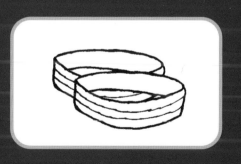 Yes? No?

helmet  Yes? No?

Word Bank

bike

mouth

eyes

skiing

glasses

sparks